The Guard Dog Geese

Roman stories linking with the History
National Curriculum.

First published in 1996 by Franklin Watts
Paperback edition published 1997
This edition 1998

Franklin Watts
96 Leonard Street
London EC2A 4RH

Franklin Watts Australia
14 Mars Road
Lane Cove
NSW 2006

Series editor: Paula Borton
Consultants: Joan Blyth, Dr Anne Millard
Designer: Kirstie Billingham

A CIP catalogue record for this book
is available from the British Library.

ISBN 0 7496 2630 5 (pbk)
0 7496 2331 4 (hbk)

Dewey Classification 937

Printed in Great Britain

The Guard Dog Geese

by
Mick Gowar

Illustrations by Martin Remphry

W
FRANKLIN WATTS
LONDON • NEW YORK • SYDNEY

Uncle Titus' villa

1

The Bad Luck Pig

Livia stood in the cool shade of the covered walkway. Although it was barely the middle of the morning, the sun beat fiercely down into the square courtyard where Livia stood. The courtyard was in the very centre of the huge, luxurious house of Livia's Great Uncle Titus.

Marcia, Livia's nurse, came hurrying through the doorway, out of the dark, cool corridor of the villa and into the open. She stopped and shaded her eyes. Livia could see that the bright Mediterranean sunlight had dazzled her for a moment. Livia could also see - even from across the courtyard -

that Marcia was looking damp and uncomfortable. Marcia was rather too plump to be rushing around in the heat of an Italian summer morning. Like Livia, Marcia preferred the thorn-sharp crispness of a British autumn, or the mild dampness of a wet British summer. She didn't like this foreign heat which felt like walking

 into a brick wall every time you got out of bed.

Marcia squinted into the sunlight. Gradually her eyes got used to the dazzling brightness which bounced off the white pillars and walls that surrounded the courtyard. She hurried round the covered walkway to the far side of the square, where Livia was waiting for her.

"Well, Marcia," demanded Livia. "What did he say? What did my Great Uncle Titus say? We can go to Ostia - *can't we*?"

Marcia let out a heavy sigh and shook her head. "I'm afraid not," she said. "Your Uncle Titus has said that it's a *bad luck day*. And that nobody's to leave the house until  a sacrifice - or something - has been made to get rid of the bad luck."

"No!" yelled Livia. "It's not fair!"

Her voice echoed along the colonnade that surrounded the beautifully kept garden.

"It's not fair!"
She screwed up her
fists so tightly that
the delicate silver
rings on her fingers
dug into her skin.
"*Why* does
everybody have to
stay indoors just
because stupid old
Uncle Titus says so?"

Ever since Livia and her parents
had arrived in Italy from Britain two
weeks before, Livia had felt trapped. Like
the garden in the centre of the courtyard,
she was surrounded, too; overwhelmed by
the enormous house, by the farm all
around it, and by all the strange grown-ups
that Livia didn't know who kept telling her

to "Sssssssh!" or "Go and play somewhere else, your Uncle Titus is trying to rest."

She hadn't so much as *glimpsed* another child in the whole two weeks they'd been living in Uncle Titus' villa. Even Uncle Titus' slaves were old and stern like him.

But today was supposed to be different. Today, Livia and her mother had planned to go to Ostia to visit her mother's cousin, Flavia, and Flavia's two daughters. But just as Livia had been

getting ready, one of the slaves had come with a message to say that Uncle Titus had commanded that no one was to go outside.

Livia had been sure it was a mistake. The slave was probably going a bit deaf - he looked old enough. But now Livia knew it was all true. The outing she'd been looking forward to so much was cancelled.

"Sssh, sssh my little dumpling," cooed Marcia. "It's a bad luck day - your Uncle Titus said so. He says that the gods are angry, and it's safer not to go outside or do anything, because anything we do might make them even angrier. And if he says that no one's to go out - then that's how it must be."

"I'm not your little dumpling!" bellowed Livia. Hot tears of rage and disappointment stung her eyes. "I hate you! I hate the farm! I hate everybody! I wish I was back in Britain!"

Livia stamped her foot down hard on the marble pavement.

"Ow!" she wailed. "Owwwww! I want to go home! I want to go home!"

Marcia put her arm around the furious child. "But this *is* your home now, Lady Livia," she said soothingly. "Your great Uncle Titus has made your father his heir. That means that one day this farm and everything your Uncle Titus owns will be your father's. And you will be a rich lady with a rich husband..."

"But I don't want to be a rich lady with a husband," said Livia fiercely.

Marcia laughed. "You will!" she said. "You will! *And* you'll get used to living here in Italy."

"Your Uncle Titus - well, he's just a bit old fashioned. He likes to follow all the old ways. But..." Marcia sighed again, "this *is* his villa and his farm. While your Uncle Titus still owns it, you have to show him respect and do as he says."

"But why did it have to be *today*?" persisted Livia. "Why did Uncle Titus decide that today was a bad luck day?"

Marcia pursed her lips, trying to control her natural urge to gossip. She looked across the open courtyard and garden, then around the colonnade that surrounded it. They were alone. She stooped down so that her mouth was close to Livia's ear.

"If you promise not to tell..." she whispered.

Livia nodded.

Marcia glanced quickly round once again.

"I heard all about it in the slave quarters," she whispered. "Last night a sow had a litter. And one of the piglets was born with five legs!"

Livia gazed at Marcia open-mouthed. "A piglet with five legs?"

"Yes," said Marcia. "That's why your

Great Uncle Titus said it was a bad luck day. As soon as he heard what had happened, he knew it was a sign!"

"A sign of what?" asked Livia, horrified and fascinated at the same time.

"An *omen*," replied Marcia, solemnly. "A sign that the gods are troubled or angry."

"And...is it still there?" asked Livia.

"Is what still there?"

"The piglet."

"Oh, I don't know," said Marcia.

Livia felt a shiver of horror run up her back as she thought of the piglet with five legs. Where was its fifth leg she wondered. At the front? At the back? In the middle of its chest? This was almost more interesting than going to Ostia. Livia made a decision - she would go and see this amazing, five-legged, bad luck pig. It didn't matter if it was a bad luck day.

It didn't matter that she was forbidden to leave the house. She was determined to see it for herself.

2

Uncle Titus and the Gods

Drusilla, Lucius and Titus stood in silence
in front of the household shrine.

Uncle Titus stared piously at the
statues in the shrine, especially at the
figure in the middle - the most important
figure, the *genius*, the spirit which

protected Uncle Titus and his farm and everything and everyone he owned.

Lucius tried very hard to follow his uncle's example, but every couple of minutes he shifted his weight awkwardly from one sandalled foot to the other. His wife, Drusilla, watched him fidgeting from foot to foot. Even though he might *look* as devout as his uncle, she knew that secretly Lucius was as bored as she was.

Drusilla remembered their own shrine in their old house in Verulamium. It had been little more than a simple framed picture of the household gods and the genius. Drusilla had tended it - more out of habit than anything else.

But Uncle Titus' shrine was magnificent. It looked like the front of a small temple, with sculpted pillars supporting a triangular top. On the platform between the pillars, stood magnificent bronze statues of the *lares* and the *penates*, the household gods, each

holding a bowl in one hand and a drinking horn shaped like a dolphin in the other. In between the lares and the penates stood the genius, a statue of a priest with his toga covering his head.

On the wall, on either side of the shrine, were wax masks of the faces of Uncle Titus' ancestors. Looking at these masks gave Drusilla a creepy feeling. They were so life-like. Uncle Titus' father, grand-father and great-grandfather staring down their long noses in disapproval, as if they'd been frozen in wax at the very moment of smelling the same bad smell.

"Silly old-fashioned superstitions," thought Drusilla. She didn't believe in all this old fashioned mumbo-jumbo. Drusilla believed in astrology. She was certain people's lives were ruled by the stars and planets, not by some outdated gods who sent ominous signs and weird messages that no one understood.

Lucius shifted his weight from foot to foot again.

Marius, Uncle Titus' secretary, hurried into the room.

"Your honour," he said respectfully, "the *haruspex* has made the sacrifice."

"Send him in, send him in!" Uncle Titus' voice sounded anxious. "We'll know for sure, now," he said, turning to Lucius and Drusilla.

"Yuck!" thought Drusilla. "A haruspex - how revolting!" Of all the old-fashioned religious rites, the one Drusilla found most repulsive was the haruspex - the special priest who examined the entrails of sacrificed animals to find messages from the gods and spirits. Drusilla couldn't hide a shudder at the thought of it.

The priest walked quickly into the room. He bowed to Uncle Titus. Drusilla felt her stomach give a lurch at the sight of his blood-stained hands. The haruspex was holding something wet and nasty which she really didn't want to see.

"I killed the lamb your honour selected," said the haruspex, cheerfully, "and the forecast is good! See - "

He walked to the small altar in front of the shrine and placed what he was carrying on the white marble. It was a liver.

"As you will see, your honour, the colour is quite normal and so is the shape. Both are good omens."

Uncle Titus' face relaxed for the first time that day. "Excellent! Excellent! I am most grateful, *most* grateful!"

The haruspex tried to suppress a grin. Titus Sextus was a rich and generous man - especially generous to those who pleased him.

"Just to make sure, you should not leave the farm today," the priest advised. "But the bad luck should be gone by tomorrow."

He bowed, and left the room.

Uncle Titus smiled. "Well, what a relief," he said. "And excellent young lamb for our meal this evening. What more could one want?"

Drusilla was suddenly aware of a movement in the doorway. "Oh, no," she thought. "Not that awful butcher-priest again!" But it was Marcia. She looked very worried.

"Marcia, what's the matter?" asked Drusilla.

"It wasn't my fault," Marcia blurted out. "I only turned my back for a minute, and she'd gone. You know what Miss Livia's

like. I've searched the whole house for her,
but I can't find her anywhere. Miss Livia
has vanished!"

"Don't be silly, Marcia," said Lucius.
"She must be somewhere in the house.
Search again. People don't just vanish.
She's probably playing hide and seek or
something. And I'm sure she wouldn't

have left the house when she's been
specially told not to -" He glanced at
Drusilla and then back to Marcia. Both
women looked worried. "- would she?"

3

Livia Escapes

Livia crept out of the deserted farmyard, through the gateway and out onto the dusty road. There was no one around to see her because of the bad luck day. In the distance she could see the twisted black trunks of the olive trees in the big

plantation. The pig sties were to the right.

Livia crouched down by the gateway. Then she began creeping along the side of the white-washed wall. She stopped and looked behind her. There was still no one about. She wondered again what might happen if she was caught. She suspected that Uncle Titus was old-fashioned enough to have her beaten if he found out she had disobeyed him.

Livia crept around the corner of the wall, and there - across a broad patch of dry, dusty ground - were the low, mud baked walls of the pig sties.

Livia stood still and stared at the pig sties, trying to gather all her courage together. She felt breathless with excitement, but it was tinged with fear. What would it look like, she wondered. Would the baby piglet be really, really horrid? She closed her eyes and tried to imagine what the five-legged piglet would look like.

She couldn't. She looked across at the squat walls surrounding the pig sties. Did she dare to go and look for herself?

Taking a deep breath, Livia began to creep across the scrubby patch of waste ground. With every step, the pig sties - with their dreadful secret - got closer and closer and...

Honk!
Hiss!
Honk! Honk!
Hisssss!

Livia let out a small shriek. Her great uncle's flock of vicious geese had appeared without warning from around the pig sty wall. Livia had been warned to stay away from them on her first day at the farm.

"They protect my farm from robbers," Uncle Titus had said. *"They're as fierce as any dogs and noisier, too. And they can't be tempted into treachery by a juicy bone or a pat on the head and a kind word!"*

But now those ferocious geese were heading straight for Livia - honking and hissing and stretching out their necks and their wicked orange beaks like gladiators practising their sword strokes and spear thrusts.

Jab!

Stab!

Honk! Honk!

Livia tried not to panic. She took two
very slow steps backwards. Where was the
slave who was supposed to look after the
geese she wondered. She'd make sure her
great uncle heard about this! Letting the
dangerous beasts wander around! Her
uncle would probably be so cross that
he'd have the slave beaten, she thought

with satisfaction.

Then she remembered - the bad luck day. There was no one outside. Everyone - including the slave who looked after the geese - had been ordered to stay indoors by her uncle. There was no one to help her. She was at the mercy of her Uncle's vicious guard dog geese.

Honk!
Hiss!
Honk! Honk!
Hissss!

The geese were now within a
couple of metres of Livia and showed no
sign of stopping. It didn't matter to them
whether she was a robber or an honoured
guest. To the geese she was something to
chase after and peck at.

Livia turned and ran.

"Help!" she screamed. "Help! The geese!"

She ran blindly across the rough uneven ground ignoring the large stones beneath the thin soles of her sandals. She looked back, hoping to see the geese far behind her. But instead of standing still, the geese were waddling after her, flapping their wings to give them extra speed.

Livia tried to force her legs to speed up. She could hear the geese honking and hissing only a few metres behind her. She could almost feel the sharp stab of their wicked beaks as they jabbed and pecked at her bare heels and ankles.

"Help!" she screamed again. "Help! Help!

Livia glanced back over her shoulder to see if the geese were still behind her, and suddenly there was no ground beneath her feet - she was falling -

Thump!

Livia landed on a flat smooth floor.
Her right leg was twisted under her.

"Oww!" she screamed. "Owwww!
Somebody help me! *Help!*"

She was trapped in what seemed to be
a small cave. It stank of something sickly,
rancid - like bad cooking oil. The stench

almost made Livia retch. She pursed her lips together, and tried not to breathe too deeply. As her eyes grew used to the gloom, she could see that the sides of the caves were smooth and pale brown. They weren't rough and rocky. A thin shaft of light was coming down from above her.

Livia looked up through the hole she'd fallen down. It was more than a man's height above her. She could just see the blue of the sky through the narrow, overgrown hole.

"I *might* be able to scramble up the sides and get out," she muttered to herself. She tried to stand up, but as she did a red hot pain shot through her left foot, the one she had landed on. Livia gasped. Tears sprang to her eyes. She bit her lip to stop herself crying with pain and fear.

She looked up at the opening again, just
as a cluster of menacing dark shadows
appeared around the mouth of the hole,
blocking out the sunlight.

Honk!

Hiss!

The geese had arrived and were

craning their necks down through the narrow opening. It was as if they'd deliberately caught her in a trap of their own making and were now closing in - honking and hissing - for the kill!

Livia screamed again.

The geese honked louder.

Again she screamed.

Again the geese honked.

Panic took her over. Livia screamed and screamed and screamed. The geese honked and honked and honked. Livia screamed and carried on screaming until a dizzy, sinking blackness swept over her.

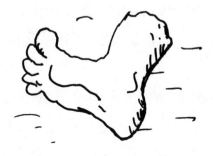

4

Livia Puts Her Feet Up

Livia sat up on the hard bed.

"You are a very naughty, very lucky little girl," her father said. "If it hadn't been for those geese making such a racket we might not have found you for hours."

Livia nodded.

"You were told not to leave the house,"
her mother added. "This is what happens to
naughty, disobedient little girls."

Livia looked down at her feet under the
thin linen cover.

"The doctor said that nothing was
broken," continued her father. "But you
had a nasty fall, so you'd better stay in bed
for the rest of the day."

"What was it?" asked Livia.

"What was what?" said her father.

"That cave I fell into."

"It wasn't a cave," said Lucius. "It was an old vat that Uncle Titus used to store olive oil in many years ago.

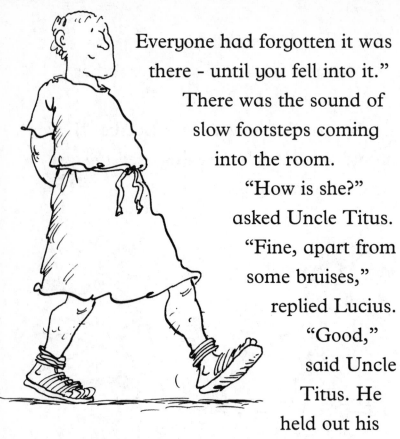

Everyone had forgotten it was there - until you fell into it."

There was the sound of slow footsteps coming into the room.

"How is she?" asked Uncle Titus.

"Fine, apart from some bruises," replied Lucius.

"Good," said Uncle Titus. He held out his hand to Livia. "You will need this child." He opened his hand. On his palm lay a small, roughly made pottery foot. It looked as if it might have been broken off a doll or a statue.

"Tomorrow morning you must give this to the gods, to show your thanks," said Uncle Titus solemnly. "But for their help, you could have broken your leg - or worse." He shook his head sadly.

Livia looked down at the little earthenware foot. She couldn't imagine that the gods would be that delighted to receive it or that disappointed not to.

Drusilla let out a quiet sigh of irritation. "More old-fashioned nonsense!" she thought. "When I get to Ostia," she promised herself, "I'm going to find a good astrologer. It's ridiculous to try and run a big household like this without an astrologer," she thought. "Almost like running it without a cook!"

Lucius was an important man, now. Important guests had to be invited to dinner. Imagine organising an important dinner party on a day when the stars foretold bad luck. Drusilla shuddered at the thought.

No, she decided. She would definitely find an astrologer. And when she did, she would ask him if today had been a bad luck day, as Uncle Titus said. Thinking of what *might* have happened to Livia, Drusilla suspected that it had been a good luck day instead.

Roman Religion and Beliefs

Gods and Goddesses

The Romans were very superstitious. By the second century, when this story is set, not many people believed in the 'old' gods and goddesses (like Jove, Juno and Mars) anymore. Instead, they worshipped new, foreign gods like *Mithras*, a Persian god who was very popular with the soldiers. Many temples which would have been used to worship Mithras have been found near forts like

the ones along Hadrian's wall and in London.
Temples usually contained treasure that had been
won in battle or had been donated by people as
a way of thanking the gods for help. *Isis* was a
popular Egyptian goddess who was worshipped
mainly by women. *Fortuna* was the goddess of good
and bad luck. Many people also believed in
astrology, which meant they thought the stars and
planets in some way affected their lives. Astrologers
claimed they could see into the future by looking at
the position of the stars at the time of a person's
birth. Sometimes emperors used astrologers to see
if they were going to be assassinated!

Household Gods

Many Romans also believed
that some gods protected their
homes. Almost all homes had
a shrine for the household
gods (the *lares* who looked
after the whole household,
and the *penates* who looked

59

after the store cupboard) which they believed
would bring good luck to their homes. The family
would visit the shrine each day to offer gifts of food
and wine. Upper class people, like Uncle Titus,
also kept wax masks or pictures of their ancestors
to make sure their ancestors' spirits were protected
(the spirits were known as *manes*). Most people
would also visit the graves of members of their
family to protect themselves against bad luck. Each
family also had its own guardian spirit, which was
known as the *genius*.

Bad Luck Days

Romans believed that lots of things were unlucky or could be unlucky. Anything done with the left hand could be unlucky. The Roman word for left was 'sinister' which we still use today to describe things which are a bit spooky, or even evil. Some days in the year were always thought to be unlucky, and on these days no work would be done and the senate (government) would not meet.

Animals and Religion

Sacrificing animals to the gods was very important to the Romans, as it was to many other religions. Animals were sacrificed at an altar in front of a temple. The ritual was very complicated and if it was done even slightly wrong then the gods would not be pleased. The Romans used priests to run the ceremony. A special sort of priest called a *haruspex* could tell if the gods were pleased or annoyed by looking at the dead body of an animal. He could tell the mood of the gods by looking at the animal's internal organs - especially the liver. If the liver did not look normal then this was supposed to mean that the gods were very angry! The animals most often used for sacrifices were sheep, goats, pigs, oxen and doves.

The Romans also believed that living animals could show the moods of the gods. Sacred chickens were kept by the Roman army. Depending on how well they were eating and crowing told the army if it was a good day to fight a battle or whether it would be better to retreat! This might be why we call someone a 'chicken' if they run away.

Villas

Romans used the word 'villa' to describe country houses like the one owned by Uncle Titus. Wealthy men who lived in the city often had a villa so they could escape to the quiet life of the country occasionally. Most villas, like the one in the story, were part of a farm. Crops were grown on the farm to make money and to feed the staff, who were mostly slaves. Crops were also used to make olive oil and wine. Villas usually had sheds to keep animals, a granary for storing grain and baths. They were built round large courtyards with beautiful decorated gardens.